The Girl

Who Wondered

What's Out There?

ISBN 978-1-0980-1195-6 (paperback)
ISBN 978-1-0980-1196-3 (digital)

Christian Faith Publishing, Inc.
832 Park Avenue
Meadville, PA 16335
www.christianfaithpublishing.com

Printed in the United States of America

The Girl

Who Wondered What's Out There?

Judy Hyman

On a blustery, gray November day, an absolutely beautiful baby girl was born in China. She had coal-black hair, creamy white skin, and expressive eyes. Her parents named her HeSha (Her-Shaw).

Despite her beauty, she was very tiny and looked fragile. Her mama and baba thought she might have medical problems, and they knew they would not be able to pay for her to see a doctor.

One night, when HeSha was about three months old, her parents made a heartbreaking decision. They called a taxi to take them to a grocery store, then they bundled their little baby up against the cold, harsh night wind. HeSha was so tiny that they were able to slip her inside a purse that her mama carried. She was fast sleep, and the taxi driver didn't even know they had a baby with them.

When they arrived at their destination, they kissed HeSha's sweet forehead and exited the car, leaving their baby wrapped up in the purse on the floor of the taxi. With tears streaming down their faces, they watched the tail lights of the taxi getting smaller and smaller as the car drove off until the lights finally disappeared.

About twenty minutes later, the driver heard soft whimpers coming from the back seat. Right away he pulled his car over to investigate what was making the sounds. That's when he saw her—a precious baby bundled up and still in the purse her mama carried her in.

In China at that time, there was a "one child per family" rule, so it was not uncommon for people to find babies that had been abandoned especially if the baby appeared to have a medical problem. Many, like HeSha, were left in plain sight so they would be found and taken to orphanages.

HeSha was a quiet baby who wouldn't eat much. Because she was so quiet, her nannies would ignore her to care for the noisier babies. She would be left in her crib while the other babies were put in baby swings to keep them quiet. Even though HeSha was lying in her crib, her eyes would follow them as they walked past her. She was watching and learning everything she could.

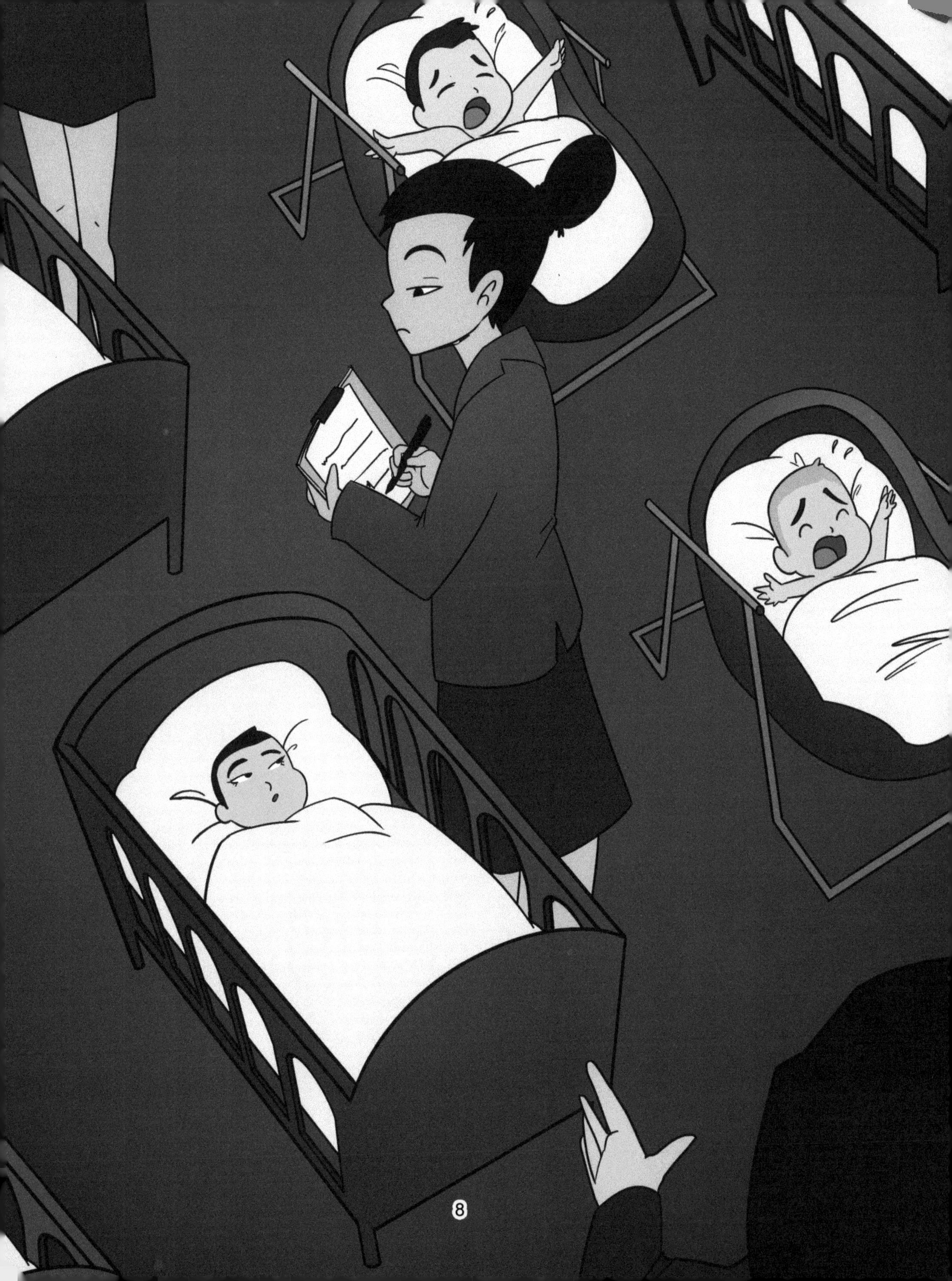

As the years passed HeSha spent hours alone in the playroom stacking blocks, softly singing to herself, and coloring.

HeSha learned that as long as she stayed quiet and well behaved, the caregivers wouldn't swat at her like they did the other kids. She also learned that the caregivers would much rather spend their time talking with each other than interacting with her or any of the other kids. Maybe if she had gotten swatted she would get the attention she was craving. But HeSha kept quiet and went unnoticed. Even though she lived with hundreds of kids, she felt very lonely.

The building HeSha lived in was very tall. Every year, on each child's birthday, they would move up to the next floor. Every floor had a large playroom with windows that stretched across three sides of the room. As the kids got older and moved up, they were able to see more and more of the city. Wow! What a sight! She had to wonder what's out there.

One day when HeSha was eleven she was overlooking over the city. The thought occurred to her that there were only two more floors left for her to move up to. She remembered all the kids she had seen move to the top floor, then on their next birthday the orphanage director, Mrs. Chang, would walk them to the front gate and she never saw them again. What happened to them? Where did they go?

One day after breakfast, HeSha was called to Mrs. Chang's office. Mrs. Chang had never showed any interest in her, so she wondered what was going on. Slowly she walked down the long hall to Mrs. Chang's office and sat in a chair in the corner. Mrs. Chang's office was very dark and HeSha was so small the chair seemed to swallow her whole.

HeSha could hear Mrs. Chang as she was walking toward her office. *Tap, tap, tap, tap* went the heels of her shoes on the cold marble floor. It seemed to take for-ev-errrr, and HeSha was getting more and more worried with each tap, tap she heard.

Finally, Mrs. Chang walked into her office and sat down behind her desk. She barely looked at HeSha, and she certainly did not smile at her. HeSha could not remember ever seeing Mrs. Chang smile.

Rather quickly, Mrs. Chang explained to HeSha that a family from Texas was adopting her and she would be leaving *tomorrow*! Wait, what? HeSha was not certain what "adoption" meant, and she certainly did not know what "Texas" meant.

She thought adoption had something to do with leaving the orphanage and going to live with strangers. Even though HeSha felt lonely and neglected, that was all she knew. Even though the nannies hardly ever talked to HeSha, they were the only caregivers she had ever known.

After leaving Mrs. Chang's office, HeSha started walking very slowly toward her room thinking about the information Mrs. Chang had just given her. One of her nannies saw her and thought HeSha looked like she was about to burst into tears. This particular nanny was the only one who seemed to care about what happened to any of the kids.

CHANG

“What on earth is wrong?” the nanny asked.

HeSha told the nanny what Mrs. Chang had just told her. She was being adopted, and she didn’t really know what that meant. HeSha also told her nanny that she was feeling confused and scared.

Upon hearing this the nanny became very excited and said, “This means you are going to have a mama and baba to love you and hug you and give you all the attention that you deserve!”

HeSha took a few minutes to think about this. Well, this changes things, but still, how can someone feel excited and scared at the same time?

Early the next day Mrs. Chang and HeSha took a taxi to a very tall building. By the time they arrived, HeSha's excitement had turned to fear. They got out of the car and walked into the building. They took an elevator up and up and up, and with each passing floor, HeSha was becoming more and more fearful.

When the elevator doors opened and she began walking toward the room where she knew her new mama and baba were waiting, HeSha started crying—*hard*! She. Was. Scared! How could she leave the only life she had ever known? The only people she had ever known? HeSha decided she could not go into that room and braced her hands and feet against the door frame. Mrs. Chang was pushing HeSha, who began crying harder and harder and louder and louder. She would not budge!

HeSha's new mama and baba looked at her with their mouths open. They did not know what to do. Finally, they approached and began helping Mrs. Chang by peeling HeSha's hands and feet away from the door frame. As soon as they would get one hand free, she would grab the door with her other hand. Mama felt like she was trying to convince a cat to take a bath!

Finally, HeSha loosened her grip and was able to just sit with Mama and Baba. They knew that they would have to sit with HeSha as long as she needed to gain her trust and realize they would take care of her.

They sat quietly for a looooong time. Then they would walk around the room for a loooong time. Finally, they showed HeSha pictures of her new home…her new room…her new pets…her new bed….After a long while, HeSha realized she was getting what she had needed her whole life—all the attention a girl could ever want.

This is not the end of the story but only the beginning of HeSha's life with her forever family.

Ten percent of the profits from the sale of this book will be donated to Chang Sha City No. 2 Social Welfare Institute in Chang Sha City, Hunan, China, which is the orphanage that HeSha spent the first twelve years of her life.

About the Author

God has definitely blessed the Hyman family! Judy and her husband, Kelley, are parents to six children. She and her husband have three adult biological sons and three daughters that they adopted from China. While Judy and her family enjoy fishing, gardening, arts and crafts and woodworking, they also make time to chill out watching movies and TV and taking plenty of naps. *The Girl Who Wondered What's Out There* is the story of their daughter, Alexis, and her time in the orphanage. Judy hopes this book will encourage people to think about the plight of orphans around the world. If you can, adopt. If you can't adopt, foster. If you can't foster, donate. If you can't donate, pray. Everybody can do something.

CPSIA information can be obtained
at www.ICGtesting.com
Printed in the USA
LVHW072341030521
686438LV00017B/331